This book belongs to

....

....

A catalogue record for this book is available from the British Library
Published by Ladybird Books Ltd.
A Penguin Company
80 Strand, London, WC2R 0RL, England
Penguin Books Australia Ltd, 250 Camberwell Road,
Camberwell, Victoria 3124, Australia
New York, Canada, India, New Zealand, South Africa

001 - 10 9 8 7 6 5 4 3 2 1

© Eric Hill, 2004
This edition published 2011
Eric Hill has asserted his moral rights under the
Copyright, Designs and Patents Act of 1988
All rights reserved
Planned and produced by Ventura Publishing Ltd
80 Strand, London WC2R 0RL

ISBN 978-0-72326-761-4

Printed in China

Spot's
Tummy Ache

Eric Hill

"Good morning, Spot!" said Mum
cheerfully. "Time to get up for
breakfast!" Spot opened his eyes.
"I don't think I want any
breakfast this morning, Mum,"
he said. "My tummy feels sore."

Mum felt Spot's forehead. "You're a little warm. I'd better take your temperature," she said. When Mum looked at the thermometer, it read normal, but she decided that Spot should stay in bed anyway.

"You need to rest until you feel
better," she said.
"All right, Mum," said Spot.

Spot snuggled back under the covers and tried to go to sleep. But he'd already slept all night, and he wasn't tired any more.

"It's boring just lying here with nothing to do," he thought.
So he got up and called Mum.

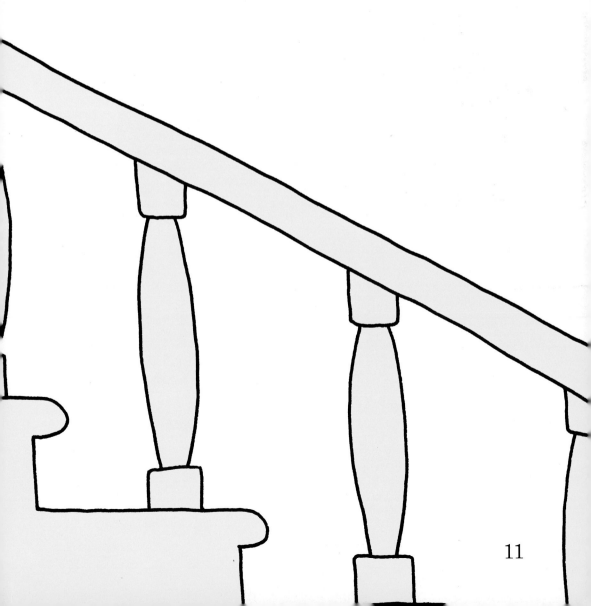

"Mum," said Spot, "would I still
be resting if I did a jigsaw?"
"Yes, Spot," she smiled. "I think
so." She brought him his favourite
jigsaw, and Spot began putting
it together.

It was so much fun he almost forgot about his sore tummy.

When Spot finished the jigsaw, he tried resting again. But it was still boring! So he asked Mum, "Can I rest and look at a picture book at the same time?"

"Yes, you can," said Mum.
She got a book from the shelf.
It was all about animals in
the jungle.

Looking at all the pictures of the hot jungle made Spot thirsty, so he asked Mum for a drink.
Mum brought him a glass of milk, and he drank it all.
"Thanks, Mum," said Spot. "Are there any biscuits in the kitchen?"

Mum laughed. "I think I can find some," she said.

Mum brought Spot two biscuits.
"Are you feeling better?" she
asked, as he ate them.
"Yes, thank you," said Spot.

"But I don't think I'm ALL better yet."
"Perhaps you need to rest a bit more then," said Mum.

Spot got under the covers and tried to rest some more. But something was making a lot of noise outside and stopping him from resting at all. Spot got up to look out of the window.

The noise was coming from Steve's garden next door. Tom and Steve were playing tag, and Helen was swinging on the swing. They were all laughing and having a very good time.

Spot's friends saw him at the window. They all waved to him. "Come and play with us, Spot!" they called.
"I have a tummy ache," Spot called to them. "But I might be feeling better soon!"

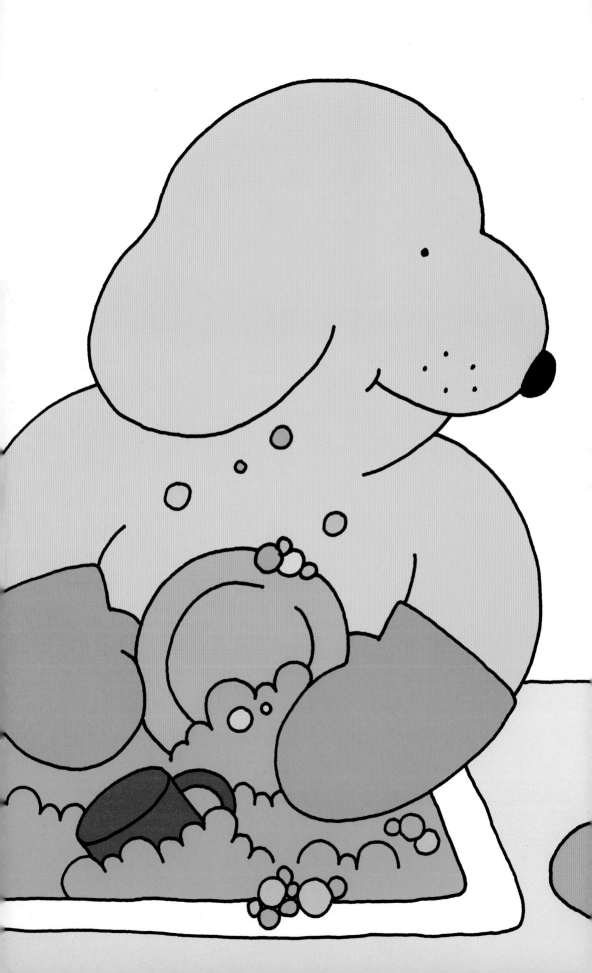

Spot went downstairs to find Mum. "I think my tummy is much better now," he said. "I can't feel the ache at all and the rest of me feels like going out to play. May I, Mum?"

"Hmmm..." said Mum. "I'm not sure. Let me feel your forehead." Spot's forehead wasn't warm anymore.
"And let me feel your tummy," Mum said.
"Tee-hee," said Spot. "That tickles!"
"If your tummy can feel a tickle," said Mum, "I think it's all better. You can go out and play until lunchtime."
"Thanks, Mum!" said Spot.

Spot ran outside and went straight to Steve's garden, where his friends were waiting for him. They all played together till lunchtime. "Having a tummy ache isn't too bad," he told his friends, "but feeling better is MUCH better!"